D0955761

GRAVITY
BUSTER

Kids Can Press acknowledges the financial support of the Government of Ontario,
through the Ontario Media Development Corporation's Ontario Book Initiative.

Published in Canada by
Kids Can Press Ltd.
29 Birch Avenue
Toronto, ON M4V 1E2

Published in the U.S. by
Kids Can Press Ltd.
2250 Military Road
Tonawanda, NY 14150

www.kidscanpress.com

Edited by Tara Walker
Designed by Karen Powers
Printed and bound in Canada

CM 07 0 9 8 7 6 5 4 3 2
CM PA 07 0 9 8 7 6 5 4 3 2 1

Library and Archives Canada Cataloguing in Publication

Asch, Frank
    Gravity buster : journal #2 of a cardboard genius / by Frank Asch.

ISBN 978-1-55453-068-7 (bound)
ISBN 978-1-55453-069-4 (pbk.)

I. Title.

PZ7.A778Gr 2007   j813'.54   C2006-905017-1

Kids Can Press is a ℓ⊙⅂⋃S™ Entertainment company

GRAVITY BUSTER

JOURNAL #2 OF A CARDBOARD GENIUS

by Frank Asch

Kids Can Press

For Eli and Tara Silver-Beattie

Table of Contents

CHAPTER 1

My Secret Identity

Right now I'm in study hall. The kid at the desk beside me is drawing motorcycles on the dust jacket of his math book. The kid behind me is memorizing a vocabulary list and tapping his foot on the leg of my chair. (So annoying!) And I'm writing with a leaky pen in a notebook I bought at Cheap-Mart for less than a dollar. I know what I'm doing doesn't look very important, but you can take my word for it: this journal is destined to become part of the most monumental manuscript in the history of mankind! Someday when it's in a museum behind bulletproof glass, even the wealthiest billionaire in the world won't be able to afford the period at the end of this sentence.

Zoe Breen, the girl who sits in front of me, just dropped a crumpled scrap of notebook paper near my left foot. After checking to make sure Mr. Howard, the study hall teacher, isn't looking in my direction, I quickly bend down and pick it up:

> Sorry, Alex, but I can't come over
> to your house today after school.
> I have to stay home and work on
> my science fair project.
> — Z

My note back to Zoe is written on a tiny slip of paper that I slide into an empty ballpoint pen and ease onto the floor so it rolls near her desk.

> That's okay. I have an IMPORTANT PROJECT
> I have to work on this afternoon anyway.
> — A

Last year Zoe won first place in the statewide Science Fair with her study of the drinking habits of guinea pigs. This year she's working with gray squirrels. She's going to offer them three different kinds of peanut butter: one salty, one plain and one sweet, and see which they like best and how it affects their health.

That's the kind of science Zoe likes. I'm more into astrophysics and space travel.

In my first notebook, *Star Jumper: Journal of a Cardboard Genius,* I described how I designed and built the world's first intergalactic spaceship. Unfortunately, I also had to give a blow-by-blow account of how that amazing spacecraft was destroyed in a senseless pillow fight with my rotten little brother, Jonathan. That's the bad news. The good news is that in the past two weeks I've been working on a new and improved Star Jumper. And it's almost finished!

My First
Spaceship

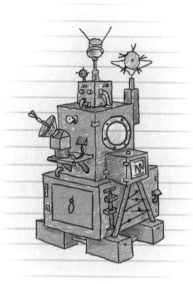

The New
Star Jumper

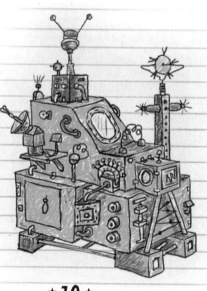

Compare the two drawings carefully. As you can see, the new Star Jumper is a lot larger, capable of carrying two passengers instead of just one. But that's the least of its new features. Notice, for example, the shoebox-sized unit duct-taped to its right side beneath the quad 4 ion-boosted radar dish. That's where the forcefield generator is located. This device is capable of erecting an invisible electromagnetic shield stronger than Superman's cape around the hull of my ship. Even a thermonuclear blast couldn't begin to dent it!

How could someone build an entire spaceship in just two weeks? Well, the fact that I work mostly in cardboard certainly helps. Cardboard is the least appreciated, most underrated building material ever invented. Not only is cardboard light, strong and easy to work with, it's free. Cardboard is also a perfect way to disguise the greatness of one's true accomplishments. I rebuilt Star Jumper in my bedroom. My mom walked past it every time she vacuumed my floor and picked up my dirty socks. But she never once suspected it was a *real* spaceship. She and my dad think it's just a toy. Something for me and Jonathan to play with. HA! He's the reason I want to leave Earth in the first place! I can't stand the thought of wasting the remainder of my precious childhood years living in the same house with that creep!

My Rotten Little Brother

A fly just landed on my hand. Now it's buzzing around Zoe's long brown hair. In case you're wondering, Zoe is really smart, but she's not a supergenius like me. She does, however, work very hard at whatever she tackles. Like right now she's hunched over her desk and concentrating so intently I can almost see smoke coming out of her ears! Hmmm ... I wonder what she's doing?

Hey Zoe, I can't see over your shoulder.
What are you working on? —A

I'm doing my math homework: adding
and subtracting fractions. — Z

I could add, subtract, multiply and divide complex fractions before I could walk. If Zoe let me help her, it would be done in two seconds.

Do you want me to do it for you? —A

No! I'll never learn if I don't figure
it out by myself. — Z

When I first decided to leave Earth I just wanted to live in a Jonathan-free zone. But that was before I got to know Zoe. Now I also want Zoe to be my co-pilot and come galaxy hopping with me. That's why the new Star Jumper is a two seater. One seat for me and one for Zoe. But so far I haven't told her the truth about Star Jumper. Like my parents, she thinks it's just a toy.

Why haven't I told her? Well, a long time ago I decided I had to keep my inventions absolutely secret. Sure, it would be fun to "go public." I can see the headlines now:

BOY GENIUS DISCOVERED:
SMARTER THAN ALL OTHER SCIENTISTS COMBINED!

Overnight I'd be rich and famous. But I'd also become a media freak. TV crews would hound me day and night, reporting on my every move. Other scientists would want to study my brain.

"How does he do it?" they would ask. "How can one person be so smart?"

Supergenius

Worst of all, the military would attempt to use my designs to make weapons of mass destruction. Ridiculous, you say? Look what happened to Einstein. The first atomic bomb was based on his formula $E = mc^2$. He tried to stop the bomb from being dropped, but nobody listened and people died! So it's not just for personal reasons that I sacrifice my own fame and fortune. It's for the good of the planet!

Einstein

The less people know about how brilliant I really am, the better. For example, I hardly ever raise my hand in class. When I do, I often give the wrong answer on purpose. On tests I make it a point to get all the hard questions wrong and always leave a few spaces blank. You might think that's dumb. But it's how I blend in. Like any superhero, I have my own secret identity. Instead of revealing my true identity — Alex, Boy Supergenius — I pass myself off as plain old ordinary Alex, an average, mild-mannered student. It's easy, really. I just *pretend* to be normal.

If I told someone about Star Jumper and he or she told someone else, even just one other person, the results could be disastrous. That person might tell someone else, and they would tell someone else, and pretty soon — well, you get the picture. The knowledge of my mind-boggling genius would spread like wildfire. The next thing I'd know the government would be knocking on my door and trying to steal my spaceship for "national security" reasons.

Clark Kent never revealed his secret identity to Lois Lane. But I intend to tell Zoe about the real me as soon as I *know* I can trust her one hundred percent. That's what my **IMPORTANT PROJECT** is all about. When I go home this afternoon I plan to complete and test my latest invention: the Trustometer.

CHAPTER 2

The Trustometer

The Trustometer is a whole new field of achievement for me. To gain the knowledge necessary to build it, I had to search the Internet and study anatomy, brain waves and neuroscience for several days. But of course no field of study is beyond my far-reaching genius.

Like all my inventions, the Trustometer is made from ordinary household items. It works on the same principle as a lie detector, recording subtle electrochemical changes that reflect the subject's inner mental states. But lie detectors merely tell if a person has told a lie. The Trustometer goes far beyond that. It reveals a person's true inner character and predicts with amazing certainty if he or she can be trusted to keep a secret.

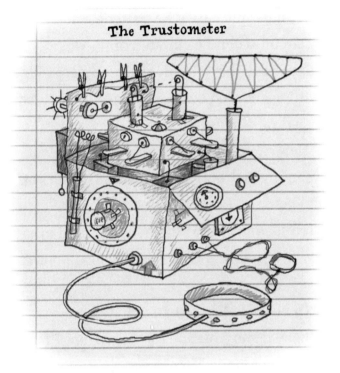

The Trustometer

Soon I'll know if I can really trust Zoe with the knowledge of my secret identity. All I have to do is hook her up to the Trustometer, ask her a few questions and analyze the results. What could be simpler? Or more brilliant?

The night the Trustometer was finished, I turned on the juice (two AA batteries) and tested every circuit. Then I calibrated brain-wave functions to within a tenth of a centimeter. When everything checked out, I was ready to proceed with tests on a live subject.

"Hey, creep!" I banged my fist on the wall between my bedroom and Jonathan's. "Get your butt in here right now, or else!"

Ten seconds later Jonathan appeared in my doorway, hands on his hips and a mean look in his eyes.

"Or else what?" he demanded.

"Believe me, you don't want to know," I said. "It could get bloody!"

"You don't scare me," he answered. "Not one bit!"

Just then the Trustometer hummed and made little bubbling noises.

"What's that?" he asked.

Like me, Jonathan is *very* curious.

"It's a Trustometer. Want to see how it works?"

"Sure," he said, and stepped into my room.

"Sit here," I said and parked him in the chair next to my desk. Then I wet his left wrist with a sponge and started to wrap the pulse receptor around it.

"Hey! What are you doing to me?" He yanked his arm away.

"Be still!" I said. "I'm hooking you up to the machine. Wet wrists will make a better connection."

"This better not hurt," he said.

"Don't worry," I reassured him. "I'm the inventor of the Trustometer. You can *trust* me."

Once the pulse receptor was attached, I slid the brain scan receiver snugly over his forehead. Then I made a few adjustments to neutralize the static electricity load.

"Ready?" I asked.

"Ready for what?"

"You'll see," I said.

I had written out some questions beforehand. "Let's say you found an envelope with a thousand dollars in it. Would you keep it for yourself or turn it into the proper authorities?"

Jonathan scrunched up his nose. "Proper authorities? What's that?"

"You know, like Mom or Dad," I answered.

"Oh, that's easy," said Jonathan. "Mom and Dad would probably waste all that good money buying something dumb like food. I'd keep it for myself and buy toys."

That was question number one. I entered the response into the Trustometer by pushing a single button and proceeded to question number two.

"Okay, let's say you're walking a dog —"

"We don't own a dog," interrupted Jonathan.

"I know, but let's say we did."

"What kind of dog?" he asked.

Like most geniuses, I'm a very patient person.

But as soon as I spend more than ten seconds near Jonathan, my patience evaporates faster than water on the surface of the sun.

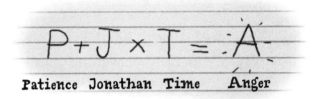

Patience Jonathan Time   Anger

"I don't know," I snapped. "It doesn't matter! Any kind of dog."

"A German shepherd!" said Jonathan. "Definitely a German shepherd. And his name is Green Paw."

This, by the way, is typical Jonathan babble: lots of words and not much sense.

"Okay," I continued. "Let's say Mom tells you not to let Green Paw off his leash but you do anyway. And let's say Green Paw runs out in the road, gets flattened by a truck and dies."

Jonathan knitted his brows and made a pouty face.

"I don't like this game," he said. "Let's play something else."

"We're not playing a game, Jonathan," I said sternly. "I'm testing you. Now answer the question."

"What question?" asked Jonathan.

"The question I'm about to ask you," I replied. "When you go home do you tell Mom you let the dog —"

"Green Paw," Jonathan corrected me. "His name is Green Paw!"

I took a deep breath and thought, *As soon as this test is over I'm throwing the creep out of here.*

"Right. His name is Green Paw." I continued, "Do you tell Mom you let Green Paw off the leash?"

"No way!" answered Jonathan. "If I did I'd get in trouble and for what? Green Paw is already dead," he added with a sad sigh.

I asked Jonathan several more questions like

these. Then I pushed the tab marked Calculate, and the Trustometer spat out the results: Jonathan, it told me in exact percentages, is completely untrustworthy. (As if I didn't know!) He also scored very low on his ability to keep a secret unless threatened with dire consequences. (Also no surprise.) So far the Trustometer seemed to be working beautifully. I was totally pleased.

"Okay, you can go now," I told Jonathan as I slid off the wristbands and head loop.

"What if I don't want to?" he replied.

"That's too bad," I said. "This is my room. You have to leave."

"No I don't," he argued. "Mom and Dad own the whole house. And that includes every room. And they're *my* parents. So this room isn't just yours. It's mine too!"

I wasn't planning on arguing with the creep. That could take hours.

"Out!" I said and pointed to the door.

Jonathan made a mean, squinty-eyed face and folded his arms across his chest.

"Okay, then," I said. "In that case, I'm throwing you out."

That's when he dove for my bed. He likes to hide under there and kick me when I come after him. Usually he's pretty quick. But today I latched onto his ankles as soon as he dropped to the floor.

"Oh, no you don't!" I hollered as I pulled him toward the door.

"I just got here," he cried. "I'm not ready to leave!"

"Oh, yes you are!" I snarled as I pried his fingers one by one from their death grip on my doorjamb.

That's when my mad dog brother bit me on the wrist! There was no blood, but he left deep teeth marks and it hurt a lot. Finally I dragged him kicking and screaming into the hall.

"Get out and STAY OUT!" I shouted.

Then I locked my door.

"Poop Head! Potty Brain!" he hollered as he pounded his little fists on the door.

Scenes like this happen all the time at my house. They almost always end up with Jonathan banging on my door and screaming names at me. Usually he gives up after just a few minutes. But sometimes he goes on and on until he falls asleep slumped against the door.

I flopped on my bed and waited for things to quiet down. That's when I had what I like to call one of my "genius moments." I had been thinking for days about ways to equip Star Jumper with an anti-

gravity device, but so far I hadn't gotten a single idea. For the first time in a long while I was stumped. Now, as I lay on my back staring up at little specks of dust

specks of dust

floating in the light of my desk lamp, the secrets of anti-gravity came to me as clearly as if someone were reading them from a book!

Why does Star Jumper need an anti-gravity device? Well, mostly to keep her from being sucked into black holes. But there are lots of ways an anti-gravity device could come in handy on an intergalactic space voyage.

You see, the bigger the planet, the more gravity it generates. That's why a person weighs a lot more on a big planet than a small one. For example, on Earth I weigh 89 pounds. On a massive planet like Jupiter I weigh 2.3 times my Earth weight, or 205 pounds. On a larger, denser planet — let's call it Planet Tubby — I might weigh several tons! Imagine what that would be like: as soon as I stepped out of Star Jumper onto Planet Tubby, I wouldn't even be able to stand up. My muscles, used to carrying only 89 pounds, just wouldn't be strong enough to support that much

weight. I'd be
pulled to the
ground and
squished into a
human pancake!

Human Pancake

And what if I crash-land on a dwarf planet?
Let's call it Planet Slim.

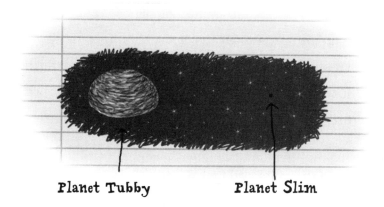

Planet Tubby   **Planet Slim**

On Pluto I weigh only 6.1 pounds. That's not very
much. On planet Slim, I might weigh no more than
a grasshopper. If I tripped on a rock or something,
I might catapult myself into outer space and never
be seen or heard from again!

That's why Star
Jumper needed this
one last improvement:
a Gravity Buster —
to control the effects
of gravity.

lost in space

I reached for my
pen the way a samurai
warrior reaches for his
sword and started jotting down one important
formula after another. I could hardly write fast
enough to keep up with the flow of my creativity.
New ideas were going off in my brain like
popcorn. As soon as I wrote down one, ten more
took its place!

Meanwhile, Jonathan was still out in the hall
screaming to get back in my room: "Big Meanie!
Banana Brain! Pee-Pee Head!"

Let him scream, I thought. *It's good for his lungs.
Maybe someday he'll become an opera singer.*

In the middle of solving a really crucial equation, I heard Mom call from downstairs, "Jonathan, you're tired and cranky. Stop bothering your big brother and go to sleep right now!"

Right on, Mom! I thought. *That's just what he deserves.*

"And you too, Alex!" she added. "It's way past your bedtime."

"Aww, Mom!" I shouted downstairs. "It's not even a school day tomorrow!"

"Growing boys need their rest," she insisted.

"Early to bed, early to rise," Dad chimed in from the den.

I can't tell you how many times I've been sent to bed because the creep is tired and cranky. It's just not fair!

Luckily, I have a simple invention for dealing with exactly this kind of situation. I call it my Thinking Tent.

CHAPTER 3

The Thinking Tent

The Thinking Tent is just a wooden yardstick and a flashlight that I keep hidden under my mattress. Whenever I need to stay up late, I prop up the yardstick under my blankets to make a little tent and turn on my flashlight. This way no light shines under my door. My parents think I'm sound asleep, and I can stay up as late as I want. The Thinking Tent has got to be my all-time simplest invention. But it's probably the one I use the most.

My Thinking Tent

After my mom came in to say good night, I set up my tent and got to work. Soon I was solving one tricky equation after another. Then, for no apparent reason, the yardstick slipped and all the blankets came down on my head.

That's odd, I said to myself. *I don't remember nudging the stick with my foot or anything like that.* But I didn't think much about it. I just shrugged and set up the tent again.

In a little while I was back to work writing down more formulas. Just as I got back in the groove, the same thing happened again. With no warning, the stick moved and down came the blankets. *Whoosh!*

Now that's really *odd!* I thought. *If that happens one more time I'm going to start believing in ghosts!*

Moments later it *did* happen again — in exactly the same way.

Then I heard a faint giggle coming through the wall next to my bed. It was just a tiny sound, but it sent shivers down my spine. It was like watching a horror movie where the monster comes back for the tenth time. *I'd know that giggle anywhere,* I thought. *The giggle of doom! The giggle from hell!*

I took a good look at my yardstick and found a strand of superthin fishing line tied to one end.

"Why, that little rat!"

I jumped out of bed and followed the string around my bedpost, across the floor, down the hall and under the door to Jonathan's room.

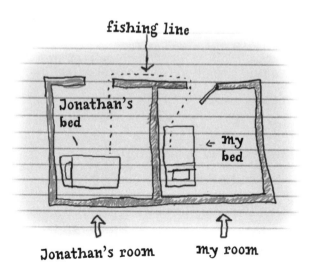

fishing line

Jonathan's bed

← my bed

Jonathan's room   my room

I flung open his door. Jonathan was curled up in a little ball like a hedgehog, snoring an obviously fake snore. As usual, he was wearing his faded old baseball cap. (He never takes it off. He sleeps with it on and even wears it in the bathtub. Mom has to fight him every time she wants to wash his hair.) His pudgy round face, rosy red cheeks and tiny pout of a mouth looked so innocent. But I knew better.

"You little creep!" I cursed and pounced on his bed.

Jonathan opened his eyes and rubbed them as if he had really been sleeping.

"Stop it!" I snarled through gritted teeth. "You don't fool me! You snuck into my room when I was talking to Zoe on the phone, didn't you?"

"Your room?" he said, still rubbing his eyes. "Go away. I'm sleeping. This is *my* room and you don't belong here!"

"From now on I want you to leave me alone," I continued. "Got it? Leave me alone or else!"

"Or else what?" he asked as a wormy little smirk slowly spread across his pudgy mug. The things Jonathan does are bad enough. But that creepy smirk pushed me over the edge. I yanked the pillow out from under his head and was about to whack him with it. I was really going to sock it to him!

Wait a minute, I told myself. *You're a scientist. Scientists are ruled by logic and reason. Not raw animal emotions!*

scientist

raw animal emotion

Instead of whacking my brother's brains out, which is what I wanted to do, I gave him the same smirk he had given me and gently set his pillow down.

"I hope you have a horrible nightmare tonight," I said through gritted teeth. "I hope hairy monsters come and eat you up at the stroke of midnight and in the morning all we find in your bed are your bones!"

I was about to go back to my room when all of a sudden Jonathan let out a bloodcurdling scream. "HELP! HELP! Alex is trying to kill me!"

"Shut up!" I cried and slapped the pillow over his face just to keep him quiet.

The next thing I knew Mom and Dad were at the door. I wouldn't hurt Jonathan. Not really. But I have to admit it certainly looked that way.

"Alex! Just what do you think you're doing?" demanded Dad.

Mom ran to Jonathan's side and held him in her arms.

"Now, now," she said. "It's okay."

Tears came sliding down Jonathan's cheeks. What an actor!

I knew I was sunk. It was the old "get Alex in trouble" trick. And I had fallen for it once again.

"It's not how it looks …" I began. But how could I expose Jonathan's treachery without giving away my Thinking Tent?

"Well?" asked Dad.

I didn't know what to say, but my rotten little brother sure did.

"He hates me … and … and … he's *mean*!" Jonathan stammered between sobs.

"Okay," said Mom. "Right now, let's all go back to sleep. We'll talk about this in the morning."

Dad scooped up Jonathan.

"Come on, Scout," he said. "You can sleep in our bed tonight."

As they left Jonathan gave me a sly little wink through his phony tears.

CHAPTER 4

The Scrambled-Egg Castle

The next morning at breakfast the creep was bright-eyed and bushy-tailed — ready to bring me new misery.

"Do you want to talk about last night, Alex?" asked Mom as she handed me a plate of scrambled eggs.

Jonathan stopped blowing bubbles in his orange juice. "It's okay," he piped up. "We were just playing."

"It didn't seem that way to me," said Dad. "We'd like to hear your side of the story, Alex."

Of course I wanted to tell my side. But I didn't dare. I couldn't say anything in my own defense without giving myself away. So I just stared down and spoke into my plate of eggs as if it was a microphone, "Jonathan is right. We were just playing. That's all."

Dad sighed. "Okay, have it your way, boys."

"Hey, Dad, look at this!" Jonathan had sculpted a big pile of scrambled eggs in the center of his plate and wanted someone to admire it.

Just then Dad's cell phone rang.

Mom sighed. "It's probably Derek."

Mom and Dad are both psychiatrists, and Derek is one of their patients. Ever since Derek's dog, FooFoo, got run over by a delivery truck last month, Derek has been suffering from severe depression.

Rest In Peace,
FooFoo

FOO FOO

Dad flipped open his phone and read the incoming number. "Yep, it's Derek. I'll take it in my office." He took a quick sip of his coffee and turned to Jonathan. "Sorry, Scout. I'll have to look at your breakfast later."

"How can you look at my breakfast later?" whined Jonathan. "It will be all gone!"

"Oh yes, well …" Dad looked confused for a moment. "Just ask your mother to take a picture of it with the digital camera and we'll talk about your breakfast at lunch."

Jonathan looked up and rolled his eyeballs. Dad yanked Jonathan's baseball cap over his eyes. Then he stood up and pushed the talk button on his cell. "Hello, Derek … yes … yes … I understand. Well … let's start with how you're feeling …" There was a long pause. "Suicidal? Mmm … that's an excellent place to *begin* …"

Dad left the table and walked to his office down the hall from the kitchen.

"Hey, Alex, look!" Jonathan turned to me and pointed to his plate. "Bet you can't guess what that is?"

"Alien vomit?" I ventured.

"Nope," he replied. "It's a scrambled-egg castle! See?" Around his "castle" Jonathan had squirted half a container of ketchup. "That's my moat," he said. "It's red because the alligators just ate some invaders."

"Bacon's ready," said Mom as she placed a plate of crispy bacon between us.

"Thanks, Mom!" said Jonathan. There were six strips of bacon on the plate. He took five.

"I can make bacon bridges with these!" Jonathan arranged the bacon in a star shape around his castle. "Now watch this! Arrrg!" He lowered his mouth to his plate, scarfed up some bacon and bit off a corner of his castle. Then he chewed with his mouth open, making disgusting animal snorts and grunts as bits of egg fell back onto his plate, his lap and the floor.

Two minutes at the breakfast table with my little brother and I was already losing it.

"Must you eat like a *pig*?" I snapped.

"I'm not a pig! I'm a mythological beast — a giant ogre!" The word *mythological* was a little too much for the creep to pronounce with all that food in his mouth. "And I eat cassstles for breakfassst!" he said as chunks of scrambled egg and bacon flew from his lips, splattering little red specks of ketchup on my scrambled eggs.

"Here. I can't eat this," I said, handing my plate back to my mom. "Jonathan just spat all over it."

"Wait a minute ..." Mom took a fork and tried to remove all the little bits of reddish egg. But she quickly gave up and scraped the whole disgusting mess into the garbage disposal.

"Don't worry, Alex," she said. "I'll make you some more eggs."

"Never mind!" I stood up and grabbed a banana from the counter. "I'll eat breakfast in my room."

Maybe it's better this way, I thought. *Now I can get to work sooner.*

"If we had a moat with a dragon we wouldn't need a garbage disposal," said Jonathan. "Just think of all the electricity *that* would save!"

As I headed down the hall to the stairs, Dad called me into his study.

"Sit down, Alex. I'll be with you in a moment," he said, cupping his hand over the phone and motioning to the big leather couch by the window.

He was still talking to Derek. "Personally, I think FooFoo still loves you," he said. "But it doesn't matter what I think. Your feelings are what count ... Why don't you think about that till our next session ..."

I sat on the stool by the door.

Finally Dad put down his cell and laced his fingers together. Then he turned his head and pointed his eyes at me like someone aiming a cannon.

cannon eyes

"I've been watching you two boys lately," he began. "And I just want you to know that I *know* what's happening."

For a moment I got really scared. Had Dad been snooping in my notebooks? Had he finally realized that my inventions weren't just toys? I swallowed and braced myself for the worst.

"What you have to understand is that Jonathan looks up to you," he said. "You're his hero, you know. He wants to be just like you."

Phew! I breathed a sigh of relief. Dad hadn't been snooping. He just wanted to talk about Jonathan.

"Well, he sure has a strange way of showing it," I said.

"He's only six, Alex. At that age little brothers want big-brother attention more than anything. But Jonathan hasn't learned yet how to get your attention in positive ways."

Yeah, but he's pretty creative when it comes to negative ways, I thought.

"I know it's unprofessional of me to offer unasked-for advice," continued Dad in his smooth-sounding therapist voice, "but if I were you, I'd try humoring Jonathan."

"You mean tell him jokes?" I said, pretending not to understand.

"Not exactly." Dad smiled. "What I'm suggesting is that you give him some big-brother time ... some attention. You'll be surprised how his behavior will change when you do. Remember the old saying 'You can catch more flies with honey than vinegar.'"

Dad loves old sayings. You would think that after years and years of higher education he could come up with something better than old sayings. Anyway, his advice made no sense to me whatsoever. Jonathan does not want my attention. He wants to torture me. His goal is to drive me crazy — absolutely insane! Maybe even have me institutionalized. Nothing more. Nothing less.

I appreciated Dad's attempt to be helpful. He means well. But mostly I just wanted to get to work on my anti-gravity device.

"Okay, Dad," I said. "I'll give it a try."

"Good," said Dad and picked up his pen. That was my signal to scoot.

So I did.

CHAPTER 5

The Quantum Sword

After my one-banana breakfast, I sat at my desk for awhile and read through last night's anti-gravity notes. I was afraid that maybe I had left out a square root or maybe even just an equal sign. Sometimes a trivial mistake like that can completely distort the results of a complex formula. But all my calculations were perfect.

Then I noticed an equation I had written in the margin of my notebook. It was just a minor leftover idea that didn't fit with my main anti-gravity concept at all. I hadn't given this "mental freebie" much thought last night. But now in the morning with a fresh brain I suddenly realized what a terrific little idea it was.

Maybe I can do something with this, I thought and started jotting down some additional notes. A few minutes later I had a

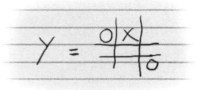

mental freebie

whole new invention on my hands! According to my calculations I had just designed the world's sharpest blade. And I wasn't even trying!

Science is like that. You're studying one thing but along the way you discover something else entirely. X-rays, penicillin, Velcro, safety glass and superglue were all *accidental* discoveries! My favorite accidental invention is the Popsicle. In 1905, when Frank Epperson was just eleven years old, he mixed a concoction of flavored soda powder in a glass of water. Then he accidentally left the glass with the wooden stick he had used as a mixer on his porch. It was unusually cold that night. In fact, the temperature dipped below freezing. In the morning Frank woke up to the world's first Popsicle! (That's why Popsicles were called Eppsicles for a while.)

The First Popsicle

Of course, that trivial invention was nothing compared to my great discovery. Theoretically, my supersword was sharp enough to slice molecules in half! Of course, a sword that sharp would be a great asset aboard Star Jumper. At the very least I could use it to defend myself against hostile aliens. But I was sure it would come in handy for lots of other purposes — like slicing open asteroids to look for minerals and drinkable water or performing delicate surgeries if Zoe or I were injured.

I was so excited. I could hardly wait to try it out! For a moment I couldn't decide what to work on first — my anti-gravity device or my supersword? Both seemed attractive. But I'm the kind of genius who likes to see quick results. And I knew the sword would take less time to finish. So I set aside my anti-gravity ideas for the time being and got to work on the sword.

I pulled out the plastic bins that I keep under my bed. This is where I store all the neat stuff I collect on garbage day. The garbage truck usually shows up by 7 a.m. But I'm always out and rummaging by 5:30 a.m. My neighbors keep me well stocked with an endless supply of old radios, tape recorders, curling irons, garage door openers — stuff like that. There's always some little thing wrong with them: a broken switch, a loose wire, etc. But that's no problem for me! I just throw away the broken parts and keep the rest.

My plastic bins are my pride and joy. Everything in them is organized in baby food jars and egg cartons. I have millions of small nuts and bolts and screws and washers to choose from. Wires, magnets, resistors, microchips — you name it and I have it. And I can always put my hands on what I need in seconds!

My Pride and Joy

As for tools? Well, I don't need many. I do most of my work with a few wrenches, some screwdrivers, ordinary scissors, lots of duct tape, a utility knife and a pair of needle-nosed pliers.

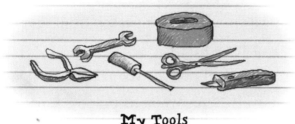

My Tools

At any minute I expected Jonathan to start pounding on my door, demanding to be let in. I don't know how he does it, but the creep always seems to know when I'm up to something interesting. And this was certainly one of those times. A half hour went by. When he still didn't show up to bug me I decided he was busy playing with Dad or something and put him out of my thoughts.

I constructed the handle of my sword with two powerful magnets taken from an old microwave oven. To this I added several modulator elements made from diodes and transistors and a quadruple inducer concocted from brass thumbtacks, a cork, a paperclip, a lead washer and four identical computer chips taken from four broken speaker phones.

The blade of my sword, like a *Star Wars* light saber, is activated only when its power source (two D batteries) is turned on. Even then, because it's thinner than the diameter of a single electron, it remains invisible to the naked eye. But that doesn't mean it's weak! Oh, no! This blade will slice through steel and diamonds as easily as an ordinary knife glides through air.

I looked around for something to experiment on. There was plenty of paper to cut. But that was too easy. I needed something no ordinary knife could handle. Then my eyes fell on the red brick that I use for a doorstop.

Perfect, I thought. *For my first experiment I'll cut that brick in half!*

I picked up the brick and put it on my desk next to Einstein's bowl. (Einstein is the name I gave my pet goldfish.)

Holding the sword over the brick, I turned on the power. *Careful,* I reminded myself. *The blade of this thing is invisible.*

Just then I felt a sneeze coming on. It wasn't the kind of sneeze that takes a long time to build up. It was the kind where you feel a little tickle in your nose and — *ACHOO!* The next thing you know, it's over. For a moment I completely lost control of the sword. When I looked down, the brick was untouched. But Einstein's bowl was sliced vertically right through the middle!

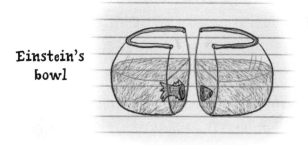

Einstein's
bowl

"Incredible!" I gasped. Both halves of the bowl had fallen apart and gently rocked back and forth on my desk. But no water had leaked out. Not a single drop! And that wasn't all. My eyes could hardly believe what I was seeing: Einstein was still swimming back and forth between the two halves!

It was the strangest, most impossible phenomenon I'd ever witnessed! Somehow my little orange fish crossed over from one side of his bowl to the other. It was so eerie to watch! When he reached the cut, Einstein's mouth seemed to disappear and then his eyes and gills and finally his tail. But, at the same time, the parts of him that had disappeared on one side of the bowl reappeared on the other!

This was a truly puzzling event. For a moment I was totally dumbfounded. My jaw actually dropped open. I'm sure I looked like an idiot.

Then my scientific mind kicked in, and it hit me. "Aha!" I cried. "The blade of my sword is even sharper than I calculated. It's so sharp that it's causing a *quantum dislocation.*"

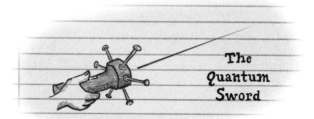

The
Quantum
Sword

I'll try to explain "quantum dislocation" as simply as I can: everything is made of atoms, right? And atoms are basically made of three different kinds of particles: electrons, neutrons and protons. The neutrons and protons stay in the middle of the atom, and the electrons swirl around in various orbits like planets around the sun. But the electrons aren't exactly like planets. Sometimes they jump from one orbit to another. Imagine Earth jumping out to Saturn's orbit and then jumping back in the blink of an eye. That's what electrons are like. The jump is measured by something called the quantum. It's an instantaneous leap. One moment the electrons are here and the next they're somewhere else. No time is involved whatsoever!

The blade of my sword wasn't just supersharp. It was *quantum* sharp! Whole atoms were jumping from one side of the cut to the other. Even Einstein's atoms were making the leap! In other words, the two halves of Einstein's bowl were separated in space but its atoms were functioning as if they were still together!

Just to see what would happen, I picked up one half of the bowl and walked around the room with it. No matter how far I separated the two halves, Einstein had no trouble "swimming" between them.

"Congratulations, Einstein!" I cried as I turned off my Quantum Sword. "You're the first goldfish ever to make a quantum leap!"

I was feeling great — basking in the scientific wonder of it all. But as I walked past my closet door, I heard the sound of snoring from inside.

"Jonathan!" I cursed.

CHAPTER 6

Footloose

I quickly picked up the two halves of Einstein's bowl and held them in place. After a second or two they automatically rebonded as if they had never been apart. Then I opened my closet door and Jonathan tumbled out.

"How long have you been spying on me?"

Jonathan belched and rubbed his eyes. "Who said I was spying?"

"What did you see?" I demanded.

"Not much." Jonathan stood up and straightened his baseball cap. "I fell asleep."

In the past I could always tell when Jonathan was fibbing to me. There was a certain guilty look in his eyes that gave him away. But lately, I have to say, he's become a pretty good liar.

"You know what will happen to you if you ever tell Mom and Dad about my inventions —" I began.

"Yeah, I know." Jonathan yawned. "You'll shrink me down smaller than a peanut and feed me to a chipmunk."

"Turn around," I said.

"What?"

"I said turn around!"

"Why?" Jonathan gave me his squinty-eyed suspicious look.

"Just do what I tell you!"

I spun him around toward the window and pulled his cap over his eyes. Then I took my key from its hiding place in the box of marbles on my desk and unlocked the door.

"Out!" I said, pointing into the hall.

"Aww, come on. Let me stay," he pleaded. "I won't be any trouble. Really. I promise!"

"And the sun goes around the Earth!" I said. "Out!"

"Please?" He looked so sad, like a droopy-eyed kitten left out in the rain meowing to come in.

Don't be fooled, I said to myself. *It's just an act.*

"Out!" I insisted.

Jonathan walked toward the door. Then suddenly he turned. He had that nasty look in his eye as though he were about to step on a disgusting bug.

Without the slightest hesitation, as if he had been planning this move all along, Jonathan snatched the Quantum Sword from my desk. Holding it tight in his little fist like a hoodlum with a switchblade, he flipped on the power.

Then he raised the sword high above his head, brought it down in a quick sweep and cut off my left foot at the ankle!

The Hoodlum

I was so totally shocked that all I could do was utter a tiny "Ah!"

There was no pain. No blood. My foot simply came off in one clean slice and fell to the floor with a clunk.

Dropping the sword, Jonathan picked up my foot and raced down the hall. Then I heard the bathroom door slam shut and a moment later the toilet flushed.

Clutching my bedpost to keep from falling, I stared at my ankle with horror and disbelief. There was no blood squirting onto the floor because it was still passing from my leg to my foot and back again — the same way Einstein had swum from one side of the goldfish bowl to the other.

The Foot Thief

And there was no pain because the nerves in my foot and leg were still "connected." So I could still feel my foot in Jonathan's hands, squeezed tight, as he ran from my room. Just before I heard the toilet flush, my foot felt wet.

Then it hit me. "Holy cosmic quarks!" I cried. "My evil little brother just flushed my foot down the toilet!"

I straightened up and steadied myself on my right foot. Then holding on to the doorknob and walls I hopped down the hall as fast as I could to the bathroom.

Jonathan was standing in front of the sink grinning up at me. He looked quite calm and satisfied with himself. It had all happened so fast that I had trouble catching my breath. I had always suspected, but now I was sure: *My little brother is a psychopath!* It seemed so obvious. I was amazed that I hadn't come to that conclusion earlier.

"In case you're wondering, I flushed your foot down the toilet," he said.

Suddenly I knew he was lying. And I didn't need a Trustometer to tell. That guilty look in his eyes was back. Jonathan was progressing nicely as a liar, but he still had a lot to learn.

"No you didn't," I said. "Where is it?"

"I told you," he repeated. "I flushed it down the toilet. If I could, I'd flush *you* down there too!"

"Where is it? Where is my foot?" I demanded.

Jonathan rocked back on his heels and looked up at the ceiling tiles as if he were counting them.

"Okay, be a royal pain in the butt!" I shouted. "I'll figure it out myself!"

I wiggled my toes. They were in water, all right. But it didn't feel as if my foot had gone down into the sewer. This water felt clean.

Then I remembered how Mom likes to soak stained clothes in a plastic basin under the sink.

I pushed Jonathan aside and flung open the cabinet doors. There in the basin on top of one of Jonathan's spaghetti-stained shirts was my left foot.

My Left Foot

I plopped myself down on the bathroom floor and reached into the basin.

Ever sleep in a funny position and have your arm fall asleep? Then you wake up in the middle of the night and it's all pins and needles and you can't move it. So you pick it up with your other hand and it feels like rubber or somebody else's hand. It's such a freaky feeling, right? Well, multiply that by a factor of a thousand and you'll have some idea of how I felt holding my severed foot in my hands.

"This better go back on!" I threatened.

Jonathan stepped back with fear in his eyes.

Very carefully, making sure to line it up right, I held my foot to my ankle. I experienced a horrible moment of doubt. What if the quantum dislocation between my foot and my leg had solidified? What would my life be like if my foot never reconnected? Would I end up carrying my foot around in a small briefcase or leave it at home on a soft pillow?

As I sat there on the bathroom floor holding my foot to my leg and wondering if I would ever have a normal life again, I looked up at Jonathan and asked, "Why did you do this to me? Do you really hate me that much?"

Jonathan just stared at me for a while with a cold, hard look in his eyes. Then he answered in a low, mean whisper, "Because you treat me like a bug. And I *don't* like it! I don't like it one bit!"

At that moment my foot reattached to my ankle. With a quiet swooshing sound I felt the parts coming together. I looked down and happily wiggled my toes. I let go of my foot and it stayed attached. Then I shook my leg and my foot stayed put.

As I rubbed my ankle, I realized there wasn't the slightest indication that my foot had ever been separated from my leg. No mark, crease or scar of any kind.

"You see?" said Jonathan. "It went back on just fine. I knew it would."

"And what if it hadn't?" I said. "I'd have to hop around for the rest of my life!"

The creep just looked at me and shrugged. "The goldfish bowl went back together."

"So you weren't sleeping, were you?"

Jonathan gave me one of his innocent-looking smiles that made me want to smack him one. I was more than angry. I was outraged. Jonathan had done a lot of nasty things to me in the past, but this was the worst yet. I stood up and he cringed.

"You hit me and I'll tell Mom! I'll tell Dad, too!" he cried. "I'll tell them all about your spaceship. I don't care what you do. I'll tell them. I swear I will!"

I was totally drained and disgusted. I just didn't want to argue anymore.

"I'm not going to hit you, Jonathan," I said with a sigh. "Just leave me alone, okay?"

Jonathan wiped his snotty nose on the sleeve of his shirt and quietly left the room.

Just then I heard Mom's office door open.

"You boys okay up there?"

"Yeah, we're fine," I muttered. "Just fine."

CHAPTER 7

The Gravity Buster

I felt like pulling out my hair and screaming, MY
EVIL LITTLE BROTHER WANTS TO DESTROY ME!
On the other hand I was overjoyed with the success
of my Quantum Sword. I felt like Frank Epperson
in 1905 contemplating the still-unknown future of
the Popsicle: double Popsicles, Fudgsicles and
Creamsicles. I was sure the Quantum Sword was
just the beginning of a whole new line of
inventions that I would someday create. Once
again I inspired myself by the raw power of my
creative genius!

But there was work to be done. It was almost
noon, and I hadn't even gotten started on my
Gravity Buster. After hiding the Quantum Sword on

a high shelf in my closet where Jonathan couldn't reach, I reread my anti-gravity notes. Then I started rummaging through my plastic bins. I must have worked for two hours straight, but it seemed like only minutes. At the end of that time I had completed my first crude Gravity Buster!

Housed in a huge cardboard box, the device was much too large to fit inside Star Jumper. But compactness could come later. First I needed to know if my basic concept really worked.

My basic concept? Well, let me put it this way: when I looked at the dust particles floating in the bright light of my desk lamp I knew they weren't really weightless. They were just tiny enough to get bumped around by air molecules. Suddenly it hit me: if gravity is caused by a tiny particle (let's call it a gravitron), then its opposite (the anti-gravitron) must also exist.

And what if gravitrons and anti-gravitrons have consciousness? What if they even have personalities?

gravitron
particle

anti-gravitron
particle

I know that sounds absurd. But I was convinced
that in all the billions and billions of anti-gravitrons
found in a single speck of matter there had to be
one, just one, willing to cooperate with me to bust
gravity and make it do my bidding. All I had to do
was find and isolate that single anti-gravitron and
help it organize other, less conscious gravitrons.
Not a simple task. But possible!

My anti-gravitron isolator was built from
bottle caps, paper clips and springs from ballpoint
pens. I upped its power load with a manifest-
transducer constructed from old wine corks and
nails wrapped in copper wire. To this I added a
trans-dimensional laser-couple that I put together

from a broken CD player and two shaving mirrors. Then came the most difficult part: the gravitron-transponder-harness. My first attempts to fashion one from paper plates wrapped in aluminum foil seemed to work just fine. But they weren't strong enough to reverse the electromagnetic thrust factor until I added two strong force/weak force stabilizers, which I made from an old bicycle tire rim and ten soupspoons.

Prototype #1

I was just getting ready to turn on the power for the first test run when Mom and Dad knocked on the door to my room.

"What's up?" I asked as I unlocked the door.

Mom looked like a movie star. Her hair was done up in a bun, and she wore high heels and a nice black dress. Dad was also dressed up, only not so successfully. His rumpled gray suit and crooked tie didn't match his scuffed brown shoes. And his hair was sticking up in a few places. Mom looked as if she was about to go to a fancy concert or something. Dad looked as if he had just stayed up all night playing poker with his friends.

"Dad's giving a talk at the college this afternoon, and I'm going along to listen and give him feedback," said Mom.

"We could get a babysitter," added Dad. "But we feel confident that you're old enough and responsible enough to keep an eye on your brother while we're gone."

I didn't want any dumb babysitter around, so I said, "Sure, I'll watch the creep."

"Thank you, Alex. We won't be far and we won't be gone long," said Mom, as she slipped her extra cell phone in my back pocket. "You know how to call if you need anything?"

"Sure," I said. "Where's the little rat fink now?"

"I wish you wouldn't call Jonathan names," Mom replied. "It may seem harmless to you, but it actually erodes his self-image."

"No need for undue concern," Dad piped up. "Alex is just venting."

Actually, I'm inventing *right now*, I thought.

"Jonathan's in his room playing in his cardboard castle," added Dad. "You know how he loves that thing. He plays in it for hours on end."

"It's wonderful that you made it for him, Alex," said Mom, as she stooped down and picked up one of my dirty socks from the floor. "It's his all-time favorite toy."

"Sure, sure," I said.

I really love my mom and dad. But right at that moment I couldn't wait for them to leave.

As I was about to close my bedroom door, Dad stuck his head back inside. "By the way, what's that you're building?"

"This?"

Dad nodded.

"It's the world's first anti-gravity device," I said. "I call it the Gravity Buster."

Mom   Dad

Dad smiled. "Clever. Very clever. Well, have fun!" He shut the door and then opened it again. "And remember what I said earlier about catching more flies with honey." He winked and shut the door.

This time, to my relief, it stayed shut.

As soon as I heard the van leave the driveway I locked my door. Then I donned some protective goggles, flipped on the Gravity Buster and hid behind my bureau.

At first the results were anything but dramatic. All the device did was shake a little. Then it made a *pocketa pocketa* sound, gave off a puff of blue smoke and just sat there.

I waited several minutes to give it time to build up a charge and re-engage. But nothing happened. Finally I got tired of waiting and came out from my hiding place. As I walked toward the device, it suddenly began to spin. I quickly jumped back behind the bureau. It spun around faster and faster until pieces began to fly out of it.

KABOOM! The entire device was scattered all over my room!

Anyone else might have considered this outcome a total failure. And in a certain sense it was. But we geniuses are used to failure. As a matter of fact, we absolutely thrive on it. *You got failure, bring it on!* That's my philosophy. We geniuses love failure because it takes us places ordinary minds never dare to tread. Living with failure is how we learn from our mistakes. And that's what success is all about.

(In case you didn't notice, the preceding paragraph contains several gems of wisdom that I'm sure people like my dad are someday going to want to quote.)

"Hey, what's going on in there?" Jonathan shouted through the wall.

"Nothing less than the March of Science!" I shouted back.

"Oh, poo!" he replied.

I picked up the pieces of my Gravity Buster and examined them very carefully until I found the problem: one of the ten soupspoons wasn't a soupspoon at all. It was a tablespoon!

"Aha!" I exclaimed. "So that's what went wrong! The tablespoon distorted the electromagnetic field matrix!"

"Hey! Quiet down in there!" shouted Jonathan.

This time I didn't bother to answer. I got right to work and redesigned everything, adding a feedback loop made from two coat hangers and a Wiffle Ball to lessen energy leakage and focus the anti-gravitrons into a steady beam. Finally, I added a remote control unit and constructed a launch pad from an old waffle iron.

At last, everything was ready.

I placed two marbles on the launch pad and began my test all over again.

This time when I turned on the machine it made a happy humming noise.

Perfect! I thought.

I picked up the remote control unit and slowly turned up the power.

One marble began to vibrate, then the other. The vibrations got faster and faster. Slowly the marbles began to rise.

"Yes! Yes!" I cried. "It's working! It's working!

Prototype #2

Am I the world's greatest genius or what?!"

"I said be quiet in there!" Jonathan banged on the wall between our bedrooms. "I'm trying to have some fun in here!"

After my first initial success I made quick progress. Each successive design got smaller and smaller and could lift bigger and bigger weights. Pretty soon I was lifting my chair and desk into the air with a Gravity Buster that could fit into a large cardboard box.

Then I built a device that could lift my bed and was small enough to fit into two shoeboxes.

From there it was a short step to my ultimate achievement: two Gravity Buster belts small enough to be worn around the waist but large enough to lift a person into the air. An elegant design, if I do say so myself!

Both belts are controlled with a single remote control device that I built from an ordinary TV clicker, a few parts from one of Mom's old curling irons and a broken vegetable strainer. Simple but effective.

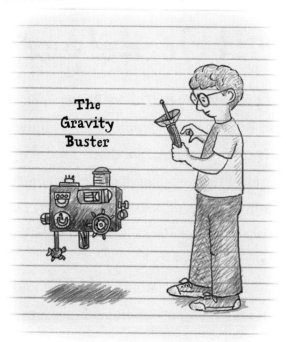

The
Gravity
Buster

Yes, it's truly incredible what you can do with a few ordinary household items and the world's most amazing brain!

CHAPTER 8

Merlin's Little Helper

I thought of testing each Gravity Buster separately by myself. But then I still wouldn't know if they worked together as a unit. Suddenly I remembered Dad's honey and vinegar advice. *Well ... what the heck?* I thought. *Lots of people actually pay Dad for his advice and I get it all the time for free. Why not try it out for a change?*

So I walked into Jonathan's bedroom and tapped on his cardboard castle with my foot.

"You in there, creep ... err ... I mean ... Jonathan?" I called, doing my best to make my voice sound pleasant and sweet.

"Go away!" he replied.

"I need some help testing something," I said.

"Would you be available for a few minutes? It won't take long."

"Is it for that stinky spaceship of yours?"

Sometimes Jonathan pretends not to be interested in my work. But I know he's *very* interested. Why else would he be spying on me all the time?

"As a matter of fact it is," I replied.

"Then I'm *busy!*"

Busy? How can a six-year-old playing in a cardboard box be busy?

"Really?" I said, still trying my best to make my voice sound more like honey than vinegar. "What are you doing?"

"I'm talking with Merlin," he answered. Ever since Mom read Jonathan a story about King Arthur and Merlin the magician, my brother won't play anything else. "Why don't you ask Zoe? She's your *girlfriend*!"

I hate it when the creep calls Zoe my girlfriend. He only says that because he knows it bugs me! Sure, Zoe's a *girl*. And she's my *friend*. But that doesn't make her my *girlfriend*!

After ten seconds talking to Jonathan, I already felt like a teakettle about to blow its lid. But I forced myself not to show it.

"I just thought you might like to help me, that's all," I replied pleasantly.

"What about Mom or Dad? Ask them to help."

"Mom and Dad are at a lecture, remember?" I reminded the little cretin. "They won't be back till dinnertime. Besides, you know I never tell them about my inventions." I was screaming now,

"SO YOU BETTER COME OUT HERE RIGHT THIS INSTANT OR I'M GOING TO GO IN THERE AND DRAG YOU OUT!"

So much for me and honey.

"No! Don't come in!" Jonathan cried and immediately lowered his cardboard drawbridge.

Jonathan crawled out, butt first, like a crab. He stood up, put his hands on his hips and made that pouty face that makes him look like the Pillsbury Dough Boy.

"Here, take this," I said and handed him one of the belts.

"What's this?" he asked.

"It's a Gravity Buster," I explained. "There are two of them. One for me and one for Zoe."

At the mention of Zoe's name, Jonathan scowled.

"It's worn like a belt," I said, and demonstrated how it straps around the waist like an electrician's tool belt.

"What's this do?" Jonathan asked, pointing to the g-force regulator on the control unit.

"Turn it up and it makes you lighter. Turn it down and it makes you heavier," I answered.

"And this?" he pointed to another knob.

"You don't need to know that," I said. "I'll be working the control unit."

"Tell me anyway," he said. "Or I won't help."

"Okay," I relented with a sigh. Nothing's ever simple with my little brother.

As I explained the basic design and function of the belts, Jonathan made lots of *mmm* and *uh-huh* sounds, but I assumed he was just pretending to understand what I was saying.

"So does it work?" he asked when I had finished.

"That's what I want to find out, lamebrain. You going to help me or not?"

"Yeah, I'll help," he said. "But you owe me a favor."

"What favor?"

"I don't know yet," he said, as he tried to wrap his belt around his waist but somehow managed to get it all tangled up.

"No, not like that, klutz!"

I finished buckling my own belt and knelt down to help Jonathan with his. I assumed he was cooperating for a change. Big mistake. As I tightened his buckle he reached past me, snatched the control unit from my back pocket and started pushing buttons.

"Hey! Give me that!" I cried.

But it was too late.

I immediately sensed a subtle vibration in the air all around us as the anti-gravity force field engaged.

This is what I get for trusting an evil psychopath, I thought. *After what just happened with the Quantum Sword I should have known better.*

Jonathan pulled down the brim of his baseball cap and flashed that demon grin of his — the one that shows all his teeth and a cruel curl to his upper lip. Then he pushed a few more buttons and we both became weightless.

Slowly our feet left the floor and we began to float up toward the ceiling.

"Give me that clicker, creep!" I reached out and tried to snatch the control unit. But Jonathan was too fast for me. He yanked the clicker beyond my reach and pushed off the bedpost with his feet, sending himself flying toward the other side of the room.

"You're going to hurt yourself!" I threatened as my head bumped into the wall. "And if you don't, I will!"

"I thought you wanted me to help you test this out?" he said, flipping with the agility of a cat so his feet hit the ceiling first.

I could hardly believe my eyes: all of a sudden the klutz is an acrobat!

While I struggled to get my bearings, Jonathan started walking around on the ceiling.

"So far, this gadget works great," he said. "Good thing I'm wearing my socks, though. Mom wouldn't like it if I scuffed up the ceiling with my sneakers."

The Upside-Down Kid

"Give me that clicker! Give it to me right now!"
I demanded.

All he gave me was another sinister grin — the ugly one that makes his nose seem to disappear.

"Let's see how it works outside," said Jonathan, and he started walking toward the open window. I had no choice but to follow. By the time I reached the window he had launched himself into the backyard and was floating about ten feet over the garage roof.

"GET IN HERE RIGHT NOW!" I shouted in my meanest voice.

"Come and get me!" he taunted.

Jonathan loves to torment me. It's a sickness with him. I was so mad. I couldn't wait to rip that control unit from his pudgy little paws. Without thinking twice I grabbed hold of the windowsill and catapulted myself into the yard.

CHAPTER 9

Falling Up

Jonathan's bedroom is on the second floor of our house so it was a good twenty feet down to the ground. But the Gravity Buster was doing its job, so of course I didn't fall. I went flying straight toward Jonathan. In another few seconds I would crash right into him. Then the clicker would be mine! Or so I thought.

By then Jonathan had totally mastered the control unit. As I came hurtling toward him, he expertly pushed another button and sent himself flying upward.

As for me, well ... I had no way of changing directions. It's basic science — the law of inertia: once a body is set in motion it continues to stay in motion until another force acts upon it.

"Wait till I get my hands on you, you rat!" I hollered and flailed helplessly as I careened over the garage roof and crashed into the lower branches of the giant oak tree that grows in the center of our backyard. Above me I heard Jonathan's sick little snorty giggle.

"Oops! Sorry," he said. "I just wanted to see if it worked outside, too. Here, I'll bring you up."

Suddenly I found myself rising through the oak, bumping into its branches as I fell upward. It was the weirdest sensation falling *up* through a tree instead of down.

"Hey! Slow me down!" I yelled. "You're bringing me up too fast!"

Either Jonathan didn't hear me or he didn't want to. I kept bumping up through the tree faster and faster, smacking into limb after limb until I finally popped out of the oak's top branches.

Free of the oak tree at last, I rose up in the air like a fishing bob rising to the surface of a pond until I was even with Jonathan — about 150 feet from the ground! Below me I could see the whole neighborhood of suburban houses and streets stretching out as far as the eye could see.

"What's wrong?" asked Jonathan. "You look mad."

"Just hand me the control unit, dweeb!" I said through gritted teeth.

"You shouldn't call me names. Didn't Mom tell you? It 'erodes my self-image.' Besides, I didn't do anything bad," he added. "I'm helping you. What difference does it make if we test out your dumb invention inside the house or outside?"

"It makes a lot of difference," I said. "What if someone sees us floating up here? How many times do I have to tell you? I have to keep my inventions totally secret!"

"I know. But look!" Jonathan pointed down to the ground. "Nobody's watching us."

He was right about that. Our house, located at the end of a dead-end street, is surrounded by tall trees. Unless someone was standing in our backyard, it would be pretty hard to spot us.

"I was just having a little fun," said Jonathan.

"Fine," I said. "Hand me the control unit and I'll forget you ever took it."

Jonathan looked at me. He looked at the control unit. Then he smiled a creepy smile. I felt as if I were watching a horror movie again — and this time the monster was about to do something *really* nasty.

"Let's go a little higher first," he said. "That can be the favor you owe me. Okay?"

"No! That's not okay!" I hollered. "For the hundredth time, HAND ME THE CLICKER!"

"Oh, you're no fun," he said and started pushing buttons again.

There was nothing I could do to stop him. We were rising slowly but steadily. Soon I could see beyond the local neighborhood to the river.

Then downtown Baxterville and the Wanatchi Mountains came into view.

Jonathan was taking in the view, too.

"It's way cool up here, isn't it?"

What he didn't notice was that we were drifting closer together.

"Yeah, really cool," I said, hoping to distract him. "See that billboard down there? Can you read what it says?"

"Mmmmm ..." He squinted a little.

That's when I made my move.

I lunged for the control unit and actually touched it with my fingertips. But at the last minute Jonathan pulled away and it slipped from his grasp.

"Oh, no!" I gasped as the control unit went flying over our heads and sailed out of the anti-gravity force field.

"Oops!" said Jonathan, and we watched as the clicker tumbled down below our feet, turned into a mere dot and disappeared.

CHAPTER 10

On the Up-and-Up

Jonathan looked at me with a sheepish grin. "I guess that wasn't good, was it?"

Wasn't good? I couldn't believe he was saying that to me.

"Do you realize what you just did?" I shouted.

"I didn't do anything!" he insisted. "You're the one who made the clicker fall.

"That's right, blame it on me," I said.

Suddenly everything went white. For a split second I thought I had

blanked out from lack of oxygen. But we weren't that high up yet. We had entered a passing cloud. The mist was so thick that when I held my hand up in front of my face all I could make out was the dim outline of five fingers.

"Hey, Alex, are you there?" said a tiny voice from the white void.

"Yeah, I'm here," I answered.

"This is scary," said Jonathan. "How are we going to get down? We can't take off the belts, can we?"

"No!" I said. "Whatever you do, don't unbuckle your belt. It will keep going up, but you'll fall like a rock. We're already too far up. The human body is seventy-eight percent water. When you hit the ground you'll end up splashing like a water balloon!"

"Splashing? I don't believe you!"

"Just try it and see."

"No thanks," said Jonathan. "What's going to happen next?"

"We'll just keep going up until the air gets so thin that we suffocate."

Jonathan's squeaky voice became shrill. "Suffocate?"

"That's right," I said. *"Suffocate!"*

The air in the cloud was so damp that little beads of mist were beginning to condense on my glasses.

"Next time you should put the controls *on* the belts," said Jonathan. "Then something like this could never happen."

"Thanks," I said as we rose up out of the cloud into the bright sunlight. "That's just what I need right now. A little design advice."

"You're welcome," he replied politely.

"Only one small problem," I continued. "There isn't going to be a next time, is there? Because we're going to *die* up here!"

"Stop trying to scare me," said Jonathan in a wobbly voice. "It's not nice."

"You've got a lot of nerve talking about what's nice," I snapped. "And I'm not trying to scare you. I'm telling you the truth!"

The air was still breathable, but I could sense it getting thinner. As the cloud drifted away we could see the ground again.

TAT TAT TAA DEE DEE TAA!

It was the sound of Mom's cell phone. I had completely forgotten about her slipping it into my back pocket before she left.

I reached into my pocket and flipped it open.

"Hello, who's this?" I asked.

"Whoever it is, tell them to send help!" cried Jonathan.

"Hello, Alex, dear," said my mom.

I held my hand over the receiver. "Shut up. It's Mom!"

"Your dad and I are having a wonderful time at the lecture. But I wanted to check in on you boys. Is everything okay?"

I thought of telling her what was happening. But the college was miles away on the other side of town. There wasn't anything she could do to help.

"Everything's fine, Mom," I told her.

"You sound a little upset, Alex," she replied. "You know how I can read your voice."

As psychiatrists, Mom and Dad pride themselves on making perfectly normal observations.

"Everything is fine," I told her.

"On the up-and-up?" she asked.

"On the up-and-up. *Really*," I told her. "I just banged my thumb with a hammer. That's all."

"Poor dear. Run it under cold water," suggested Mom. "Can you put Jonathan on the line, please?"

"Ah … he's taking a nap."

Mom suddenly sounded concerned. "In the middle of the afternoon? He's not running a fever, is he? Did you feel his forehead?"

"Yeah, Mom, and he's fine. He's just tired from running around the house playing cops and robbers."

"Cops and robbers?" protested Jonathan. "I never play cops and robbers! I play knights and wizards."

"Hold on," said Mom. "Your dad wants to say something."

"No, not now!" I wanted to get off the phone real bad. The air was already so thin that I was starting to feel out of breath. "I … I … I have to go soak my thumb."

"You do that, dear," said Mom. "Your dad and I will be home —"

"Okay! Bye, Mom!" I said and hung up.

The cell phone! Why didn't I think of that? How could I have forgotten about it? At the time I thought it was a dumb idea. But now I realized it was our only hope!

Our Only Hope

"Awww! Why did you hang up?" whined Jonathan. "I wanted to talk to Mom!"

Jonathan started to go on and on about never seeing Mom or Dad or his castle again and how it was all my fault that he was going to suffocate before celebrating his seventh birthday.

"Oh, shut up!" I snapped and started dialing.

CHAPTER 11

The Peanut-Butter Scientist

Zoe's phone rang six times before she picked up.

"Zoe Breen," she said. Her voice was cheerful and upbeat. Zoe almost always sounds happy, as if she's just won a prize or something.

"Look, Zoe, a big problem has come up and I need your help right away," I said without wasting a moment's time. "It's sort of an emergency. Can you come over right now?"

"This is Alex, right?" said Zoe.

"Yes! It's me. Can you come over to my house?"

"Are you okay?" she asked. "If you're bleeding or something you should call 911."

"It's not that kind of emergency."

I was working hard to stay calm, but my voice

sounded shrill. "Can you come?"

"I'm coming right now," said Zoe. "You mind telling me what's up?"

"*I* am," I said.

"What?"

"Never mind," I said. "I'll explain when you get here."

We were already pretty high up. So high up that the entire town of Baxterville stretched out below us like a miniature railroad set. I could hardly tell one house from the next, but Jonathan insisted he could still see our house and Zoe's as plain as day.

"It's that one there," he said, pointing between his feet. "The one with the black shutters. And see that little blue dot. That's Zoe. She just pulled out of her house on her bike."

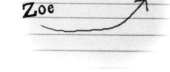

Jonathan has eagle eyes, which kind of makes sense when you think about the fact that eagles are predators.

"Zoe, are you still there?"

There was static followed by silence and a clanking noise. Then Zoe's voice came back.

"Yeah, still here," she said. "You want me to hang up?"

"No, no! Don't hang up," I said. "Are you on your bike?"

"Yeah, how did you know?" she answered.

"We can see you," I said. "We're about two thousand feet above you. Two thousand feet and rising."

"Her bike just stopped," said Jonathan.

I strained to see what Jonathan was seeing but couldn't make out a thing.

"Look, if this is some kind of joke I don't have time for it right now," said Zoe. "When you called I was just typing up the results of my latest peanut-butter experiment and —"

"No, it's not a joke. We really need your help," I pleaded. "You're our only hope to get back down."

"Are you in a hot-air balloon or something?" asked Zoe.

"Not exactly," I said. "But that's close."

"She's just pulling into our driveway," announced Jonathan.

"What do you want me to do?" asked Zoe.

"You have to find something that fell in the backyard," I said and described the control unit.

"Do you have any idea where it landed?"

"It could be anywhere," I said.

"Tell her to look in Mom's flower bed," said Jonathan.

"Did you see it go there?" I asked.

"Sort of," he answered.

"Check the flower bed by the back fence," I said.

control unit

flowers

A few moments later Zoe reported back. "I found something weird sticking straight up in the mulch. What *is* this thing?"

"The control unit to our Gravity Buster belts!"

"The *what?*" exclaimed Zoe.

"Never mind," I said. "Just handle it carefully and do exactly what I tell you, okay?"

"Sure," she said. "What do I do first?"

"See the red button," I instructed. "Whatever you do, don't turn it off."

Suddenly there was lots of static on the line.

"What did you say? Turn it off?"

"No! DON'T turn it off!" I shouted. "D-O-N-T as in DO NOT! Got it?"

"Got it," said Zoe.

I could tell she felt a little offended.

"Sorry," I said.

"That's okay," she replied.

I gave Zoe careful step-by-step instructions to bring us down.

First I told her to switch us on dual command with the TV/video button. Then I had her lower us slowly down toward the ground by alternating between the volume and the channel buttons, starting with nine and working backward to one.

"Phew!" I let out a sigh of relief. Zoe did everything just right. *She's going to make a terrific co-pilot,* I thought.

"Hey, it's working!" cried Jonathan. "I knew you'd come up with something. You always do!"

I looked over at Jonathan and he was smiling at me. Just then I saw something in his eyes. It only lasted for a second. Then he looked away. It could have been admiration or maybe even something more than that. *Could Dad be right?* I wondered. *Did Jonathan worship me? Was I really his hero?*

Brother Worship

CHAPTER 12

Photo Finish

Pretty soon, as we descended through some small clouds, I could see Zoe standing in our backyard. In one hand she held the control unit. In the other she held her tiny point-and-shoot camera. (Zoe never goes anywhere without it because she's always on the lookout for a photo of an interesting plant or insect.)

"I can hardly believe what I'm seeing!" she cried. "Alex! What are those crazy contraptions you're wearing?"

"The world's first Gravity Busters," I answered.

This was *not* how I had planned to reveal my secret identity to Zoe. But there was no point in testing her with the Trustometer now. She already knew too much.

"Gravity Busters! Alex, that's *incredible*! I just can't believe it!" she said, pointing her camera at us.

"Wait! Stop! What are you doing with that?" I called down.

"Taking your picture," she replied.

"No, don't —" I tried to stop her, but the next thing I knew the flash went off in my face.

"Wow!" she cried. "This is so awesome. No, it's more than awesome — this is *historic!*"

"Zoe, quick, nudge the volume dial up a notch," I said, noticing we were coming down a little too fast.

She turned the dial and our descent slowed to a crawl until we were hovering about twenty feet above the ground.

Suddenly I had an idea. I instructed Zoe to lower me all the way to the ground. Then I grabbed the clicker from her and stopped Jonathan's descent.

"Hey, I want to come down, too!" complained Jonathan as he continued to hover twenty feet above the lawn.

"Not yet," I said. "You need to ponder the wickedness of your evil ways first."

Jonathan immediately launched into a midair temper tantrum, kicking and screaming with all his might.

"You can't do this!" he cried. "Get me down!"

"Just returning a favor," I said.

"GET ME DOWN! GET ME DOWN *RIGHT NOW!*" screamed Jonathan.

"Come on," I said to Zoe. "It's kind of noisy out here. Let's go inside."

Zoe looked up at Jonathan grimacing down at her. "What about your little brother?"

I did feel a slight pang of guilt. After all, if it wasn't for Jonathan, Zoe might still be looking for the clicker in the backyard. His eagle eyes really did save the day. Then again, Jonathan was the one who had caused all this trouble in the first place.

"Oh, don't worry about Jonathan," I told Zoe. "I'll bring him down in a little while. But first I want to show you something really important."

"This is so incredible," gushed Zoe as we walked toward the house. "Wait till the world finds out about your Gravity Buster. You're going to be the most famous person on the planet!"

"Yeah, I know. My Gravity Buster *is* incredible," I said. "But the world's not ready to find out about it

— or me! So everything I show you today has got to be kept *absolutely* secret."

Zoe looked at me as if I were crazy. *"Secret?"* she said. "Are you serious? This is news, Alex! Big news! World news! You're going to be on television and —"

Me on TV

"No I'm not," I said. "Because you're not going to tell anyone. Not even your parents."

"I'm not?"

"No. You're not," I insisted. "And you have to promise or I won't show you any more of my inventions."

"You have more?" she gasped.

"Lots more," I said.

Jonathan was still screaming bloody murder. *"GET ME DOWN! GET ME DOWN!"*

Zoe looked back. "Maybe we should do something about Jonathan first?"

"Oh, he'll be all right," I said. Then I caught her eyes and held them in my gaze. "So, do you promise?"

Zoe swallowed.

"Yeah, sure. I promise," she said.

As we stepped inside the house Zoe noticed that I was shivering.

"It was really chilly up there in the stratosphere," I said and grabbed a sweater from the hall closet.

"You should eat something, too," suggested

Zoe. "That will put some more calories in your system and warm you up faster."

That was a sound scientific observation, I thought. *Zoe* is *going to be an excellent partner in outer space.*

Detouring through the kitchen, I took some granola bars from the pantry and offered one to Zoe.

"No thanks," she answered. "I've been eating peanut butter all day."

All of a sudden I was starving. I inhaled two granola bars in the kitchen and then a third as I led Zoe upstairs to my room.

"Get ready," I said as I opened my door. "You are about to set eyes upon the greatest scientific achievement in the history of mankind!"

CHAPTER 13

Journey to Jupiter

Star Jumper is about the size of a small swing set. It reaches from the edge of my desk all the way to the closet door, taking up most of the extra space in my bedroom.

"Well, here it is," I said.

Zoe looked puzzled. "Ah … errr … Alex, I've seen your spaceship before. And I think it's really nice that you made your brother such a fun toy to play with, but ..."

Suddenly I saw the light go on in Zoe's eyes as if someone were shining a flashlight from inside her brain.

"You mean … this … this is a *real* spaceship?"

"Just as real as anything NASA ever built," I said as I unbuckled my Gravity Buster and set it on my desk. "And more advanced. *Way* more advanced!"

Zoe just stood there and stared, wide-eyed and speechless.

"Let me show you around," I said.

I opened the main hatch and climbed inside.

Zoe hesitated, but only for a second. She looked as if she were thinking, *Am I dreaming or what?*

"This is the cargo hold and engine room," I said, and switched on a small light so Zoe could get a better look. But the light didn't go on.

That's odd, I thought. *I just changed the batteries for that light last week.*

Zoe cleared her throat. "I can't see much."

I reached for the small penlight I had duct-taped near the hatch for just such an emergency and clicked it on.

"Is that better?" I asked.

"A little," she replied.

"This is where we'll store all our food and stuff," I said, opening two separate doors to the storage bins. "This is for your things. And I'll put mine in here."

"*Our* food and stuff? What stuff?" asked Zoe.

"You know, stuff — clothes, toothbrush, soap, books, CDs — personal stuff. And of course any research gear you might want to bring along. After all, I assume we'll be encountering lots of interesting alien specimens in our travels. You'll want to bring along plenty of notebooks and batteries for your camera and some research equipment to do field studies. Come on, I'll show you the command center. That's where we'll sit most of the time. It's a lot roomier up there."

"You're inviting me to go into outer space with you?" said Zoe, as we climbed the ladder to the upper half of the ship.

"You bet I am," I answered. "I want you to be my co-pilot."

In addition to the ship's main computer, control console and viewer portal, the command center was outfitted with two homemade chairs constructed out of cardboard and some old pillows

I found in the attic. The pillows had pink roses on them, but they were plenty comfortable.

"Everything in this ship is made of reinforced cardboard and can tolerate above-normal levels of acceleration," I said, as I pounded my seat with my fist. "But of course we'll be traveling mostly in Quantum Mode. There won't be any stress on us or the ship at all."

Zoe sat down in the chair beside mine and took a careful look around.

Instead of her usual excited self she was strangely quiet.

"This is actually my second spaceship," I said. "The first one was pretty basic. The Stellar Drive worked on the same principle. But it was only half as large as this one and lacked some very important features."

"Important features?" asked Zoe. "What important features?"

"I'm glad you asked," I replied. "Let's say we want to know if the air on a particular planet is breathable or not. All we have to do is push one button and my Interplanetary Spectrometer will tell us the chemical composition of its atmosphere in a matter of seconds! Neat, huh?"

Gee, I'm starting to sound like a salesman trying to sell someone a car, I thought.

Zoe just nodded.

"Actually, the Interplanetary Spectrometer is one of my least original inventions. Other scientists have designed similar devices. But building it from soup cans, bent nails and toilet paper rolls — now that took some smarts!"

Once I got started singing Star Jumper's praises, I couldn't stop.

"As you know, space travelers are likely to encounter harmful viruses and bacteria for which they have no natural antibodies," I continued. "A potentially lethal problem. But Star Jumper is equipped with a fully automatic Astral Inoculator, which I put together mostly from old vacuum cleaner parts and a coffee maker that someone left out for the trash man. Focus its laser ion beam anywhere on the planet in question, and this amazing device will analyze the microbe situation and concoct a remedy for any potential disease. Wait a few minutes, then flip a switch and a little white pill will drop into a Dixie cup. All we have to do to be totally protected from any alien microbe is swallow that pill with a little water."

The Astral Inoculator

Zoe looked a trifle pale. I guess this was a lot to take in.

"Also aboard this ship, in addition to a highly effective Asteroid Repeller,"

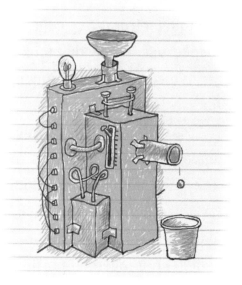

I continued in my best car-salesman-like manner, "is the most amazing telescope ever invented. I made it from tin cans, cardboard tubes and several broken Coke bottles. It's no bigger than a pair of oversized binoculars but so powerful it allows me to see completely around the universe! As Einstein predicted, the universe is curved. So with this telescope I can look out one end and see the back of my head with the other!"

Zoe wasn't saying much. She looked kind of stunned.

"Incredible, huh?" I said. "I guess it's hard to believe that the kid sitting behind you in study hall is the greatest scientist of the twenty-first century."

Zoe took a deep breath and said, "So you're telling me this is a *real* spaceship, and it can orbit the Earth and —"

"Orbit the Earth, nothing!" I exclaimed. "This baby can hop from one galaxy to the next as easily as a frog jumps from one lily pad to another."

"And you're asking me to be your co-pilot," she stated flatly.

"Yep."

"Ahhhhh … Alex …" Zoe's tone of voice told me I was not going to like whatever she said next. "I know I saw something amazing just a little while ago. Something truly incredible. But it's hard to imagine myself going into outer space with you in a cardboard box."

"Sixteen cardboard boxes in all," I corrected her. "All reinforced."

"I mean …" she continued, "I think what you've done here is really great … err … I mean, if it really works the way you say it does … But look what just happened to you and Jonathan. If I hadn't been home working on my science project when you called, where would you be right now?"

Suffocating to death somewhere in the stratosphere, I thought. But I kept my mouth shut about that.

Things sure weren't going the way I thought they would. I expected Zoe to be totally thrilled when I told her the truth about Star Jumper. Then it occurred to me: *Maybe she needs a demonstration!*

"How about a little ride?" I asked. "We don't have to go far. Just to Jupiter and back."

"*Where?*"

"To Jupiter. We could go and be back in a matter of minutes!"

"Wouldn't it take longer than that just to get this ship out of your bedroom?" asked Zoe.

"Nope," I boasted. "This spacecraft is equipped with an Atom Slider. All I have to do is flip this switch over here and the Atom Slider will generate a force-field vortex that will allow us to pass right through the ceiling and roof of this house." I flipped the switch to show her.

"This spaceship goes through *walls*?" she exclaimed.

"That's right," I said, and turned the dial that

fully engaged the Atom Slider.

Slowly we began to rise up off my bedroom floor toward the ceiling.

"Alex!" cried Zoe. "What are you doing?"

"Just showing you how the Atom Slider works," I said, revving up the cross-generator defibrillator.

Zoe's expression was the same as when she first saw the Gravity Buster in action: total wonderment.

Star Jumper felt a little tippy, so I adjusted the gyros.

"Don't worry, we'll stabilize in a moment," I said.

Zoe leaned forward and peered out the portal. "We're floating!" she cried.

"Uh-huh," I said and turned up the power level half a notch. "We're just in Maneuver Mode now. When the ship's in Jump Mode she moves the way an electron leaps from one orbit to another in an atom. Instantly. First she's here. Then she's there. Distance doesn't matter. Once you master one jump, you can keep jumping as fast and as far as you want to."

Zoe managed a smile. "Is that why you call her Star Jumper?"

"You got it!" I said, and pushed the final sequence button. In less time than it takes for a gnat to blink, Star Jumper leaped 685 333 000 miles from my bedroom into an orbit several miles above the surface of Jupiter.

Suddenly we both got very quiet. For what seemed like a long while, though it was probably only a few seconds, we just sat and stared out the portal. I felt like a tiny bug hovering above a giant, living jewel.

Jupiter is so huge that if it were hollow, about one thousand Earths could fit inside. It rotates faster than any other planet in the solar system, making a complete revolution in slightly less than ten hours. That rotation causes Jupiter to bulge out at its equator. The planet's atmosphere, composed mostly of hydrogen and helium, turned beneath us like a huge color wheel broken up into ribbons of rich, vibrant colors. It truly was the most beautiful sight either of us had ever seen!

"Oh wow," said Zoe at last. "This is so lovely. I can't believe you don't want the whole world to see what we're seeing!"

in orbit, miles above Jupiter

"Someday, sure," I answered. "But right now I don't want strangers poking their noses into *my* business."

"You don't want to go on TV?"

"And be interviewed by a bunch of stupid news reporters who don't know an electron from an election? No way!"

"But this is so special! *You're* so special! Like … Leonardo da Vinci! Like Einstein! Your genius belongs to the world!"

I was thrilled to hear Zoe compare me to Einstein. After all, he's my hero.

Just then I heard a faint giggle coming from the cargo hold. It was only a tiny sound, but it sent shivers down my spine. *I'd know that giggle anywhere,* I thought. *The giggle of doom! The giggle from hell!*

I set the controls on automatic pilot and climbed down the ladder to the cargo hold.

Zoe was right behind me.

"Did you hear that?" I asked.

"It sounded like laughter," she said.

I opened the hatch and turned on the penlight. This time I made a careful inspection. Wedged between boxes of spare equipment and a backpack full of extra notebooks was the top of Jonathan's baseball cap.

I reached out and grabbed the cap.

Suddenly Jonathan's head popped up. He gave me a nasty look as if I should be ashamed of myself for disturbing him. Then his face lit up with an evil grin.

Once again my rotten little brother had outsmarted me!

Somehow when I was in the kitchen with Zoe eating granola bars he must have drifted over to the house and climbed in my bedroom window. Then he had slipped into Star Jumper and hidden in the cargo hold. He'd even thought to remove the batteries from the light so we wouldn't see where he was hiding. *Crafty little creep!*

"I'm taking you home right now!" I snapped.

"Good," said Jonathan as he snatched his hat back. "But first help me get out of here. I want to see Jupiter, too!"

Good News, Bad News

I'm sitting in study hall again. The kid beside me is drawing speedboats today. The kid behind me is memorizing his French spelling list and *still* kicking the leg of my chair! (I *really* wish he'd stop!) And I'm writing on the last few pages of this notebook, which by now you must agree really *is* part of the most monumental manuscript in the history of mankind!

Zoe, by the way, was very impressed with our visit to Jupiter. Of course, we didn't stay long and we didn't go down to the surface. Jupiter has a rocky core of metallic hydrogen surrounded by liquid hydrogen, so there wouldn't be much to see down there anyway. No life whatsoever — not even basic algae.

But there will be plenty more interesting places to visit once we leave the solar system. I want to meet alien creatures as smart as or maybe even smarter than me! Then there will be lots of cool ideas and inventions to bring back to Earth. Or maybe I can help aliens with *their* problems!

The good news is that Zoe has agreed to be my co-pilot! So everything is all set in that department. Boy, am I relieved! But she isn't ready to leave quite yet. Zoe wants to wait till after she finishes her peanut-butter squirrel experiments and enters this year's Science Fair. (She says she doesn't care if she wins, but I think she does.)

And the bad news? Well, I had to promise to take Jonathan with us when we leave. It was the only thing I could think of to make sure he didn't squeal to Mom and Dad. He was so jealous when he found out that Zoe is definitely coming with me. He didn't even wince when I threatened to destroy his castle if he tattled on me.

But just because I promised to take Jonathan with me doesn't mean I really have to. Zoe and I could always just sneak away in the middle of the night when he's sound asleep.

Zoe says she doesn't mind if Jonathan comes along. She says she always wanted a little brother and he's "kind of cute." Of course, she doesn't know him that well yet. Just wait. She actually thinks she can teach him some table manners. I think she'd have more luck teaching sea lampreys to tap dance!

tap dancing sea lampreys

On the other hand, anyone reading this journal will have to admit Jonathan is one clever kid. And he's small. It wouldn't be difficult to outfit a place for him to sleep in the cargo hold. "Give up your mission to drive me crazy and I *might* consider making you a member of the crew," I said when I "promised" to take him along. Since then he's been on his best behavior. But, of course, Jonathan's best behavior doesn't go very far.

That night, for example, when we returned from Jupiter, Mom and Dad invited Zoe to stay for dinner.

"We got some Chinese on the way home," said Mom. "You wouldn't care to join us, would you, Zoe?"

Jonathan got so excited about the idea of eating Chinese food he flung out his arms and legs as if he was a firecracker going off. Dad, who was holding Jonathan at the time, got slapped in the ear and kicked in the groin.

"Oh, wow! I love Chinese food!" Jonathan exclaimed. "Especially those little crackers that look like baked worms. Did you get me chop suey?"

"Yes." Dad winced as he set Jonathan on the floor. "We got you chop suey."

"How about fortune cookies?"

"We got fortune cookies, too," said Dad. "And they gave us an extra that can be Zoe's."

"How about it, Zoe?" asked Mom. "Would you like to stay for dinner?"

The last thing I wanted was to have Zoe witness the primitive spectacle known as "Jonathan Eating."

Please! Please say no! I prayed. But apparently the Higher Universal Force was not listening to my prayers at that moment, and if it was, it was not relaying the message to Zoe.

"I'd have to call my parents first," said Zoe.

"Didn't you say your mom was cooking your favorite dish and you couldn't wait to go home for dinner?" I lied, nodding my head up and down, hoping Zoe would catch my drift.

Zoe looked at me funny.

"No, I didn't say anything about dinner," she replied, "but I think we're having leftovers tonight. And I *love* Chinese food."

"Good," said Mom. "Make your call. I'm sure it will be okay. I'll set an extra place at the table!"

As I predicted, dinner was absolutely horrific.

Jonathan, of course, dined in his usual disgusting manner: mouth wide open so everyone could observe the grinding action of his sharp little teeth.

I must say, Zoe seemed to handle it all very well. When Jonathan stuck mung bean sprouts up his nostrils like long dangling boogers, she calmly offered him her napkin.

"Do you need to blow your nose?" she asked.

He grinned and said, "Thanks."

mung bean
boogers

dangerous
Jell-O

I think she won him over right then and there.

He took the napkin and pretended to blow his
nose, making a loud honk that a Canada goose
could be proud of. Then he began to separate all the
components of his chop suey. Bamboo shoots here,
bean sprouts there, baby corn over there. When he
had everything in neat little piles he lowered his face
to his plate, stuck out his lips and sucked in each
little pile like a human vacuum cleaner.

It was truly gross and noisy.

When Mom put dessert, a dish of green Jell-O, in front of Jonathan, he shook the plate until the Jell-O wiggled. Then he screamed, "LOOK! IT'S ALIVE!" and proceeded to stab wildly at it with a chopstick until he declared it was "not dangerous anymore!"

That night we all got fortune cookies after dinner. Mine read, "You are about to go on a very long journey."

You bet, I thought. *And the sooner the better!*

Blast off with more chapter books from Kids Can Press

Alex, the self-proclaimed Cardboard Genius, is able to build a spaceship, an anti-gravity machine and even a time machine — so why does he always seem to be at the mercy of his rotten little brother, Jonathan? Complete with the Cardboard Genius's many top-secret blueprints, Alex's journals make for cosmically hilarious chapter-book reading. Written and illustrated by acclaimed children's book creator Frank Asch.

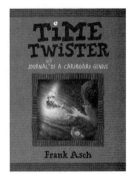

HC ISBN: 978-1-55337-886-0
PB ISBN: 978-1-55337-887-7

HC ISBN: 978-1-55453-068-7
PB ISBN: 978-1-55453-069-4

HC ISBN: 978-1-55453-230-8
PB ISBN: 978-1-55453-231-5